Sophie Dau

By Tennant Redbank

First published by Parragon in 2012
Parragon
Queen Street House
4 Queen Street
Bath BA1 1HE, UK
www.parragon.com

ISBN 978-1-4454-4746-9

Printed in China

# Hide-and-Seek

## A little story for little learners

Bath • New York • Singapore • Hong Kong • Cologne • Delhi
Melbourne • Amsterdam • Johannesburg • Auckland • Shenzhen

Pixie Hollow was quiet and still.

No fairy wings fluttered.

No fairy voices filled the air.

Where had all the fairies gone?

Suddenly,

along came Tinker Bell.

She flew alone

over a garden.

Tink pulled up close to a tall tulip.

Rosetta peeked out
from behind some petals.
They were playing a game
of fairy hide-and-seek.
And Tinker Bell was IT!

Tinker Bell still had so many fairies to find. There was Rani and Nettle, Fira and Silvermist, and Iridessa and Fawn. Beck was usually easy to spot. She couldn't stay still for long. But Prilla was very good at hide-and-seek. It might take Tink a while to find her.

Tinker Bell looked behind
a spiderweb.

She checked under a pine cone.

She peeked into a knothole.

Then she saw a bright light.
It was shining from
behind a leaf.

Only one fairy glowed
that brightly.
"Fira!" Tink yelled.
Tink pulled the leaf back.
There she was!
"You found me!" Fira said,
giggling. Tink couldn't stay
to talk. She had other
fairies to find!

Tink found Silvermist
behind a rainspout.

She spotted Fawn
in a bird's nest.

Iridessa was trying to blend in
with the fireflies.

Nettle was hiding in an old cocoon.

Tink fluttered around a stone.
On the other side,
she found Rani,
a water-talent fairy.
Rani was playing
with a water ball.

"I've got you!" Tink shouted.

Rani jumped. She was startled.

She dropped the water ball.

It burst into a hundred droplets.

Tink had a game to finish,
so she flew into the woods.
"I can't believe I haven't
found Beck," she said.
Up ahead, she saw a flash
of colour. Tink flew closer.
It was a red-spotted toadstool.
But wait...
something was behind it.
Maybe it was Beck!

It wasn't Beck.
But it was a red-haired
fairy in a green cap.
"Prilla!" Tink shouted.

Tink told Prilla who
she had already found.
Tink wondered how
many more friends
she had to find.
She said goodbye to
Prilla and flew away.

Tink scratched her head.
She was stumped!
Beck was usually
the easiest fairy to find.
Today Beck was not just
an animal-talent fairy –
she was a master hider!

Tink was about to yell
"Come on out, Beck!"
But before she did,
a soft sound reached
her ears. It seemed
like a breath.
Or a whisper.
Or...a snore!

Tink followed the noise.

It was coming from a hollow log.

She poked her head inside.

There she found

Beck curled up

with a family of hedgehogs!

"Beck! You are the last
    hide-and-seek fairy!" said Tink.
"I am?" Beck asked.
"How nice!"
    She snuggled back in
    with the hedgehogs.
    Soon Beck was asleep again.

Tink was tired after
all that looking.
Maybe a little nap…
Before Tink closed her eyes,
a voice called "Tink? Beck?
Where are you?"
Another game had begun!